LAKE SUPERIOR

CANADA

Sault Ste. Marie

MICHIGAN

LAKE HURON

LAKE MICHIGAN

Big Bay de Noc

N
W E
S

Clever Beatrice

A note from the author: Contes and Conteurs

The upper peninsula of Michigan is rich and varied in the tradition of regional Native-American and European folktales, including the Canadian *conte*. Like the Finns, Swedes, and Irish, French-Canadians were lured to northern Michigan by the lumber boom of the late 1800s. Canadian *contes* were told originally in lumber camps and iron mines and were known for wild exaggerations, comic detail, and rhythmic dialect. *Clever Beatrice* is an amalgam of several stories about voyageurs making bets with rich and powerful giants. I broke somewhat with tradition by making my protagonist a clever, persistent girl, and named her after my French-Canadian mother-in-law, the late Beatrice Joanisse, herself a fine and funny *conteur*.

To my Joanisses
—M.W.
For Kelen May
—H. M. S.

First Aladdin Paperbacks edition September 2004

Text copyright © 2001 by Margaret Willey
Illustrations copyright © 2001 by Heather Solomon

ALADDIN PAPERBACKS
An imprint of Simon & Schuster
Children's Publishing Division
1230 Avenue of the Americas
New York, NY 10020

Also available in an Atheneum Books for Young Readers hardcover edition.
Designed by Sonia Chaghatzbanian
The text of this book was set in Goudy.

Manufactured in China
10 9 8 7 6 5 4 3 2 1

The Library of Congress has cataloged the hardcover edition as follows:
Willey, Margaret.
Clever Beatrice / written by Margaret Willey ;
illustrated by Heather Solomon.—1st. ed.
p. cm.
Summary: A small, but clever, young girl outwits a rich giant
and wins all his gold.
ISBN 0-689-83254-0 (hc.)
[1. Folklore—Michigan. 2. Tall tales.] I. Solomon, Heather M., ill.
II. Title.
PZ8.1.W648 Cl 2001
[398.2]
[E] 00-042019
ISBN 0-689-87068-X

Clever Beatrice

AN UPPER PENINSULA CONTE

by Margaret Willey   illustrated by Heather M. Solomon

Aladdin Paperbacks
New York   London   Toronto   Sydney

Sure, she was little, but Beatrice loved riddles and tricks and she could think fast on her feet. "Sharp as a tack," her mother said. The neighbors would wave to her as she passed by and say to each other, "She's a clever one, that Beatrice."

One day her mother put a bowl of porridge in front of Beatrice and said, "Eat, eat, my girl, but not too fast. This is the end of our porridge." Her chin trembled as she sat down to her own small bowl.

Beatrice ate slowly, thinking of how she might help her mother. Finally she said, "It is time for me to go out into the far north woods and get some money."

Her mother sighed. "There are only two ways to get money up here," she said. "One way is to cut down the trees with the lumberjacks, but that is not work for little girls."

"What is the second way?" asked Beatrice.

"There is a giant on the other side of the woods," her mother said. "A rich giant who loves to gamble on his own strength." She sighed again. "But you are only a little girl, you."

"Is the giant smart?" Beatrice asked.

"When you are a rich giant," her mother said, "you do not have to be smart."

Beatrice thought about this.

The very next day, she kissed her mother good-bye and walked away from the village into the deep woods, through a forest of white pines and copper hills, farther than she had ever walked before. Finally she came to a wall of pine trees at the bottom of a hill where she watched some lumberjacks sawing down the biggest tree of all. Just as the tree fell down—*whoosh-bang!*—the lumberjacks called out "Day's over!" and waved good-bye to Beatrice. Beatrice waved back and then kept walking, all the way up the hill.

At the top was a huge log cabin. Beatrice found the giant
sitting against the side of this cabin, taking in the late afternoon
sun. She came straightaway beside him and said in her loudest,
bravest voice, "Good afternoon, Mister Giant, Sir. I have come
to make a bet with you."

The giant opened one eye and looked down at Beatrice.
"What kind of a bet from such a little girl?" he asked.

Beatrice took a step closer and made a fist no bigger than a
walnut. "I bet ten gold coins," she said, "that I can strike a blow
harder than you."

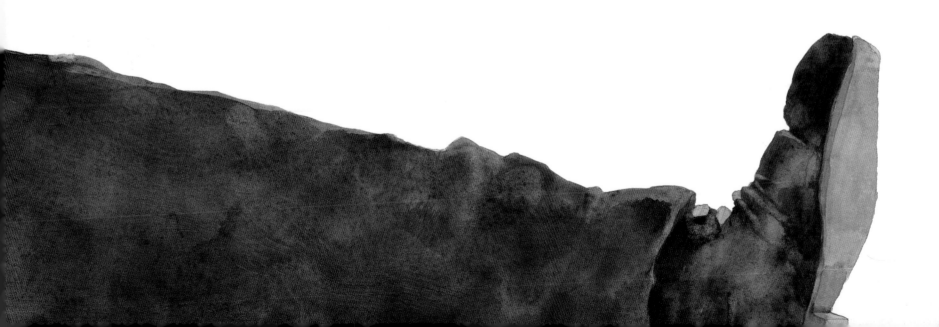

The giant thought this was very funny. He stood up and laughed, showing off his height and belly. Then he made a huge fist with his own hand and held it next to Beatrice's. "What should we strike with our mighty fists to make our bet?" he asked.

Beatrice looked at the giant's cabin and pointed to his front door, a door as big as a boat, made of long planks of pine. "Let us strike against your front door, we two. The hardest blow will win the bet."

"Oh, you are making a big mistake, you," the giant chuckled. He walked over to his front door, swung his arm back, and then let his fist fly hard against the wood—*ker-blam!* The walls trembled, the windows rattled, the door groaned on its brass hinges. The giant turned and grinned at Beatrice, showing all his teeth. "Your turn," he said.

Beatrice stepped up to the front
door, turned to the giant, and said,
"Don't worry if I break your door, Mister
Giant, Sir. See what happened to that
pine tree down there?"

"What tree?" the giant asked.

Beatrice pointed to the broken tree at
the bottom of the giant's hill and said,
"That great big knocked-over one, there."

"You did that?" the giant asked.

"Well, I thought you might need a tree for
your new door."

The giant frowned and scratched his head.
"Maybe I don't want a new door," he said.
"Maybe I like my old door."

"I'm sorry, Mister Giant, Sir," said
Beatrice. "I am only trying to win the bet."
She raised her fist at the door.

"Never mind, you!" the giant cried.
"Don't break my door! I would rather just
give you the money."

Beatrice said, "If you insist."

The giant gave her ten gold coins. He was not one bit happy about it. He walked outside the cabin behind Beatrice, shaking his head. "Let us have another bet, we two," he said. "We will go down to my well and carry back some water for my stove. If you can carry more water than me, I'll give you ten more gold coins. But if I carry more than you, you must give me back my money."

"I accept," said Beatrice. When they reached the well, the giant filled many buckets with water, six on each arm.

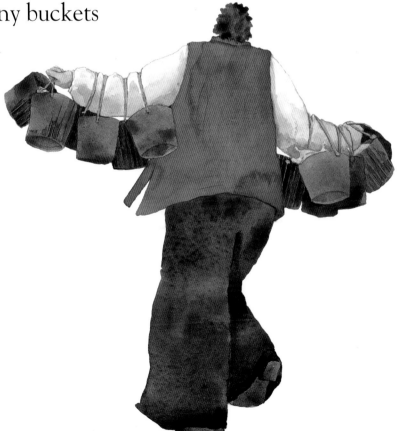

But Beatrice took a big rope from beside the well and began to wrap it around the well, around and around.

"What are you doing?" asked the giant.

"I am not going to bother carrying those buckets one by one," Beatrice said. "I would sooner pull out the whole well."

"But if you pull out my well," the giant cried, "then I will not be able to get water for my stove!"

"I can't help that, Mister Giant, Sir," Beatrice said. "I am only trying to win the bet."

"Leave the well where it is," the giant said. "It is not worth losing my water."

Beatrice said, "If you insist."

The giant gave Beatrice ten more gold coins, but he was even more unhappy about it. He scratched his head and tugged his beard and then led Beatrice farther into the woods until they came to a clearing where a huge iron bar lay on the ground.

"Let's have another bet, we two," the giant said, pointing to the bar. "If you can throw that thing farther than me, I'll give you ten more gold coins. But if you cannot throw it as far as me, you must give me back all my money."

Beatrice said, "I accept."

The giant picked up the iron bar and stood in the middle of the clearing. He stopped, turned around twice, let out a bellow, and threw the bar a good two hundred feet into the air. *Whoosh-wham!*—it fell to the ground. Then he looked at Beatrice with a smile. "Your turn," he said.

Beatrice was too small to even pick up the iron bar. She walked over to where it lay on the ground and crouched over it, thinking hard. Then she stood up and pointed to the east and asked the giant, "Do you know anyone who lives in Canada?"

"I have some brothers in Sault Ste. Marie," the giant replied. "They like the wind and the snow up there."

Beatrice turned to face Canada and cried out in her loudest voice: "BROTHERS OF MISTER GIANT! I AM GOING TO THROW THIS BAR YOUR WAY—WATCH YOUR HEADS!"

"No, no!" said the giant. "Don't throw the bar that way. I do not want to get in trouble with my brothers."

"What about this way?" Beatrice asked, pointing west.
"I have some brothers over that way, too," the giant
said. "They work in the copper mines, over by Wisconsin."

Beatrice faced west and cried: "BROTHERS OF MISTER GIANT! I AM GOING TO THROW THIS BAR YOUR WAY—WATCH YOUR HEADS!"

"Not that way!" cried the giant. "I don't want to get in trouble with those brothers, either."

Beatrice pointed south,
toward Big Bay de Noc.

"I have some brothers
who fish in that bay!" the
giant exclaimed.

Beatrice faced south and cried: "Brothers of Mister Giant! I am going to throw this bar your way!— Watch your heads!"

"Not in the bay!" the giant cried.

Beatrice pointed north. "But if I throw the bar back this way, it might land right on the roof of your cabin."

The giant held his head.

"I'm afraid I have run out of places to throw the bar," said Beatrice.

"Never mind," said the giant. "It is not worth getting into trouble with any of my brothers."

"Then I've won again, Mister Giant, Sir," Beatrice said.

"Here, here, take the rest," said the giant. He gave her his last ten gold coins in a silver bag.

"Thank you, Mister Giant, Sir," Beatrice said.

"Go home, little girl," the giant said. "You have cost me a fortune. But at least I didn't have to make a new door."

"That's true," Beatrice agreed.

"And I still have my water and I didn't get into trouble with my brothers." The giant sat back down in the sun beside his cabin, smiling to himself, feeling lucky.

Beatrice backed away, taking slow steps.
Only when she was far along on the path
from his cabin did she break into a run. Only
when she was in sight of her mother's cabin
did she let out a yell. She held up the silver
bag with the gold coins inside, waving to her
mother. She could not wait to tell her how
she had bet three times against the strength
of a giant and three times won.

Her mother would say
that Beatrice was the most
clever girl in the whole
north woods. Beatrice could
not wait to hear it.

WISCONSIN

LAKE
SUPERIOR

CANADA

Sault Ste. Marie

MICHIGAN

LAKE
HURON

LAKE
MICHIGAN

Big Bay de Noc

N
W   E
S